MY LiFe
as a
Haunted Hamburger,
Hold the Pickles

Tommy Nelson® Books by Bill Myers

Series

SECRET AGENT DINGLEDORF
. . . and his trusty dog, SPLAT 𝄪

The Case of the . . .

Giggling Geeks • Chewable Worms
• Flying Toenails • Drooling Dinosaurs •
Hiccupping Ears • Yodeling Turtles

The Incredible Worlds of Wally McDoogle

My Life As . . .

a Smashed Burrito with Extra Hot Sauce • Alien Monster Bait
• a Broken Bungee Cord • Crocodile Junk Food •
Dinosaur Dental Floss • a Torpedo Test Target
• a Human Hockey Puck • an Afterthought Astronaut •
Reindeer Road Kill • a Toasted Time Traveler
• Polluted Pond Scum • a Bigfoot Breath Mint •
a Blundering Ballerina • a Screaming Skydiver
• a Human Hairball • a Walrus Whoopee Cushion •
a Computer Cockroach (Mixed-Up Millennium Bug)
• a Beat-Up Basketball Backboard • a Cowboy Cowpie •
Invisible Intestines with Intense Indigestion
• a Skysurfing Skateboarder • a Tarantula Toe Tickler •
a Prickly Porcupine from Pluto • a Splatted-Flat Quarterback
• a Belching Baboon • a Stupendously Stomped Soccer Star •

The IMAGER CHRONICLES

The Portal • The Experiment • The Whirlwind • The Tablet

Picture Book

Baseball for Breakfast

www.Billmyers.com

the incredible worlds of **Wally McDoogle**

MY LiFe
as a
Haunted
Hamburger,
Hold the Pickles

BILL MYERS

Tommy NELSON

A Division of Thomas Nelson Publishers
Since 1798

www.thomasnelson.com

Published in Nashville, Tennessee, by Tommy Nelson®, a Division of Thomas Nelson, Inc. Visit us on the Web at www.tommynelson.com.

Tommy Nelson® books may be purchased in bulk for educational, business, fund-raising, or sales promotional use. For information, please email SpecialMarkets@ThomasNelson.com.

Scripture quotations in this book are from the *International Children's Bible*®, *New Century Version*®, © 1986, 1988, 1999 by Tommy Nelson®, a Division of Thomas Nelson, Inc. All rights reserved.

Library of Congress Cataloging-in-Publication Data

Myers, Bill, 1953–
  My life as a haunted hamburger, hold the pickles / Bill Myers.
      p. cm.— (The incredible worlds of Wally McDoogle ; 27)
    Summary: Having made a bet on whether or not ghosts are real, Wall Street and Wally, aided by Opera and Madame Mystic, investigate a house on the edge of town that might be haunted, although Wally has learned why the Bible says to avoid the occult.
    ISBN-13: 978-1-4003-0636-7 (pbk.)
    ISBN-10: 1-4003-0636-1
    [1. Haunted Houses—Fiction. 2. Occultism—Fiction. 3. Christian Life—Fiction. 4. Humorous stories.]
    I. Title.
PZ7.M98234Myef 2006
[Fic]—dc22

                                                    2006016251

Printed in the United States of America
06 07 08 09 10 RRD 5 4 3 2 1

For Dee Ann Grand:
A woman with vision
and a heart for the children.

"Do not go to mediums or fortune-tellers for advice."

—Leviticus 19:31

Contents

Chapter 1

Just for Starters

The next time I sneak in to see an R-rated movie, just put a sign across my forehead that reads:

WARNING:
- ☐ Moron Under Construction
- ☐ Toxic Waste Site
- ☐ Brain Transplant Needed Here

(Please check appropriate box.)

Of course, Mom and Dad don't let me see that junk. I have to get a presidential order signed in triplicate just to see a PG-13. But when your best friend knows a friend who knows a brother who works at the ticket window . . . well, there are ways.

Unfortunately, there are always ways.

So there I was, watching the scariest movie of my life: . . .

BODY-STEALING GHOSTS FROM JUPITER

Actually, I was doing a lot more *non*-watching than watching—it's kinda hard to watch anything when you're under the theater seat, praying for your life, and getting your face stuck to the floor on somebody's old Gummi Worms. (Don't you just hate it when that happens?)

Look, it's not that the movie was scary, I'm just not a big fan of ghosts from another planet stealing humans to put in their petting zoos back home (although I hear the food is great).

Anyway, after more screaming, shrieking, and body-stealing than any alien life form should be allowed, the movie finally came to an end.

"Was that cool or what!" Wall Street (my best friend, even if she is a girl) said after the paramedics restarted my heart for the third time, and we headed home.

"Ab, *munch-munch,* so, *crunch-crunch,* lute *burp,* ly!" Opera, my other best friend, said while working on his ninth barrel of popcorn with extra butter. (Hey, you can't blame him just because they give free refills.)

"I don't know," I said, checking the sky for any low-flying UFOs whose occupants might be looking for bodies. "I thought it was pretty gross."

"Yeah." Wall Street grinned.

"BURP!" Opera burped.

"I'm not so sure," I said, glancing over my shoulder. (Sometimes alien life forms like to sneak up from behind.)

"C'mon, Wally," Wall Street said. "It's not like that stuff is real or anything."

"BEL—" Opera started to belch, then stopped. "It's not?"

"No way," she said. "Well, except for the ghost part."

"There's no such things as ghosts," I said, ducking from a lightning bug. (Sometimes alien spacecraft like to disguise themselves as insects.)

"What about that haunted house outside of town?" she asked.

"Haunted?" I gulped.

"Gulp?" Opera gulped.

"Sure," she said. "Weird stuff always happens there. You know, like ghosts, goblins, the usual sort of haunted stuff."

"There's no such things as ghosts," I repeated.

"You tell them that."

I shook my head. "You're letting the movie get to you."

"I am not."

"Are too."

"Am not."

We could have kept that in-depth conversation going forever had Wall Street not hit me with, "If you're so sure you're right, then you won't mind giving me money when I prove you wrong."

I know, I know, I should have immediately run for cover. Who needs body-stealing ghosts when they have money-stealing best friends?

My point is, whenever Wall Street uses the word *money*, three things happen:

1. Warning bells go off in my head.
2. I grab my wallet.
3. I give up and just hand over the cash.
   (She plans to make her first million by the time she's fifteen and so far, all of it has been off me.)

Since I was still brain-dead from the movie, I stupidly stuck out my hand and, though betting is definitely uncool, even stupidlier (Don't try that word in English class.) shook her hand.

(You'd think after twenty-six books I'd know better. I guess that's why we're doing number twenty-seven.)

"Great!" She grinned, which meant I was in trouble. "Meet me at that haunted house, eight o'clock tomorrow morning, and I'll *prove* to you there are ghosts."

She broke into a chuckle, which meant I was really in trouble.

She threw herself on the ground, rolling back and forth in uncontrollable laughter, which meant I should probably just give her all the money in my bank account *and* my folks' credit cards. Because if there is one thing Wall Street doesn't know how to do, it's *not* make money . . . especially off me.

* * * * *

The good news was, the movie didn't affect me at all. I mean, other than:

—The seventeen nightmares.
—Never setting my bare tootsies on the floor again. (They say body-stealing ghosts love hiding under beds.)
—Never sticking my head out from under the covers for the next month . . . or two.

Of course, there was the minor problem of breaking into hysterical screams every time I heard strange and mysterious sounds—like my chattering teeth, my knocking knees, or my whimpering between breaths.

But, other than that, everything was great.

I did need something to unwind a bit, though. And what better way to relax than to work on one of my superhero stories. So, after grabbing Ol' Betsy, my laptop computer, and pulling her under the covers, I went to work.

It had been another long, hard day of superherodom for Manners Man. Already he had:

1. Stopped a superjock from throwing a gigageek into the showers (at least while he was carrying his Blackberry, XBox, and electronic chess game).
2. Convinced a teen girl to stop rolling her eyes at her parents every five seconds. (Now she's up to every twelve seconds—talk about progress!)
3. Then there was that thing about bringing peace to the Middle East (which was small potatoes compared to #1 and #2).

At last he sits down with his family for a nice turkey dinner when suddenly

a giant ghost from Jupiter appears
above their house and stomps them
flatter than some bug playing tag with
our windshield on the freeway.

Wait a minute, that's not right. This is supposed to be a superhero story, not some stupid
ghost story. Who would write stupid ghost stories, anyway?

(Certainly not me.)

I hit DELETE, stuck my head out from
under the covers for a quick breath of fresh air,
and tried again.

It had been another long, hard day
of superherodom for Manners Man. At
last he sits down with his family for
a nice turkey dinner, when suddenly a
thousand lost souls of the dead rush
up out of the kitchen-sink drain. They
scream, shriek, and do all those
annoying lost-soul types of things, as
they prepare to turn the family into
mindless zombies who—

No! No! No! Come on, McDoogle, think!
I hit DELETE and tried again.

Manners Man sits down with his family for a nice turkey dinner, where there are no ghosts (especially large ones who stomp houses) and absolutely no lost souls hanging around inside kitchen plumbing.

"Please pass the mashed potatoes," Perfect Daughter with perfect teeth says.

"Why, certainly, dear," Perfect Mother, who never raises her voice, replies.

"Oh, please, allow me," Perfect Son, who never teases his sister, insists.

I paused a second and looked at the story. Needless to say, I was grateful that I'd finally gotten all that horror stuff out of my head. So, after taking another breath of air outside the covers, I went back to work.

"Manners Man," Perfect Wife asks, "would you carve the turkey for us?"

"Why, I'd love to," he replies.

He sticks the turkey with the carving fork and is about to begin slicing, when suddenly the bird leaps up off the platter. It wrestles the fork from Manners Man's hands, jumps onto the back of his chair, and holds the fork against the man's neck—making it clear that if anyone moves, Manners Man will be a goner.

"What's happened?!" Perfect Wife cries.

"It's the turkey!" Perfect Son shouts. "It's been possessed by an alien spirit!"

"No doubt from Jupiter!" Perfect Daughter screams.

"Don't worry!" Manners Man yells. "Just don't let them steal your body or—"

I hit DELETE.

Where did all these ideas come from? Got me.

I shut Ol' Betsy down and lay under the blankets. Of course, I wasn't able to sleep—not with all the junk running through my head.

So, I decided to just lie there.

Night wouldn't last forever. In just a few terrifying hours, daylight would finally arrive and my fears would be gone.

Soon, Wall Street, Opera, and I would get back together.

Soon, my life would return to normal. Well, at least normal for me—which, as we all know, is far scarier than any nightmares or ghosts from Jupiter.

Chapter 2

Cookies and Caskets

The next morning I arrived at the so-called haunted house more than a little nervous.

I would have been less than a little nervous if, when I pushed open the front gate, it didn't

K-REEEAK . . .

and

GROOOAAN . . .

like some Jupiter spacecraft opening up, waiting to eat me alive.

I would have been less than a lot nervous, if it weren't for the half-dozen coffin-sized boxes stacked up on the porch next to the front door.

And I probably wouldn't have nearly passed out . . . if it weren't for the talking bush beside that porch!

"Hey, Wally!" it hissed.

I opened my mouth and gasped.

Not only was the bush talking, but it was also growing a head right out of the top of it.

And not just any head . . . Wall Street's head!

"What did you do with the rest of her?!" I yelled.

"What?" it asked.

I gave another gasp. Not only had it sprouted Wall Street's head, but now it was speaking through her mouth!

"Spit her out!" I shouted. "Spit her out this instant!"

And sure enough, just like that, the bush spit Wall Street out of its side. (Funny, she wasn't even wet from all those nasty digestive bush juices.)

"What are you talking about?" Wall Street demanded. Apparently, she was in such shock she didn't even remember being eaten.

Then, as a bonus prize, it spit Opera out its other side.

But before we had a chance to celebrate, Opera pointed up at the attic window and cried, "L-l-l-look!"

We spun around, looked up, and saw a tall old guy in a tuxedo. He stood on the roof just outside a second-story window.

Weirder still was that he wasn't totally solid. We could actually see part of the window through him.

And weirder stiller was that his long gray hair and tuxedo were blowing in a hurricane-force wind.

The only problem was, there was no hurricane.

Come to think of it, there was no wind!

He looked down at us and scowled. Then he raised his arm and pointed his long bony finger. Suddenly, being eaten by a bush didn't seem like such a bad idea.

But before I had time to leap into it for cover, the old man opened his mouth and screamed.

Only there was no sound.

Instead, his entire body started to shake and vibrate.

Soon, giant chunks of his hair started falling off and blowing away.

Then his face started blowing off . . . until it was nothing but a skull. (Talk about a weight-loss program.)

But he wasn't quite done. The next thing to blow away was his tuxedo . . . immediately followed by the rest of his skin and muscles.

Now he was nothing but a skeleton.

But a very angry skeleton, who was still pointing and yelling at us . . . until he suddenly collapsed into a giant heap of bones that any dog would go nuts over.

I was scared in a major *do-I-want-to-run-off-screaming-hysterically-or-just-fall-down-dead-and-avoid-the-rush* kind of way.

Of course, my friends were equally as scared, which would explain Opera turning to us and shouting, *"B-b-b-b-burp!"*

And Wall Street turning to me and asking, "W-w-w-ill you be paying off that ghost bet by c-c-cash or c-c-redit?"

Before I could answer, or at least have a couple of good fainting spells, I heard a loud

K-SCREEECH.

I turned toward the noise and saw the front door opening. A hunched-over lady with white hair stepped onto the porch.

"YOU!" she yelled at us.

Of course, we should have been polite and answered . . . but it's hard remembering your manners when you're busy tripping over each other, racing to the front gate, and pushing on it for all you're worth.

But our worth wasn't worth much because the gate wouldn't budge!

"We're trapped!" Opera cried.

"Guys!" Wall Street shouted.

"Like rats in a trap!" I yelled.

"Guys!"

"LIKE POTATO CHIPS IN ONE OF THOSE PLASTIC BAGS YOU CAN NEVER OPEN!" Opera screamed.

"GUYS!"

"WHAT?" we yelled in two-part harmony.

She yanked our hands off the gate and, instead of pushing, simply pulled it

K-REEEAK . . .
GROOOAAN . . .

open. (When a guy's dying he can't think of everything.)

"Children!" the old lady shouted. "Children!"

Against our better judgment, we looked back over our shoulders.

In her hands was a giant plate of freshly baked chocolate chip cookies.

But we aren't fools. We continued through the gate. No way would we fall for that old trick. No way would we—

"Opera!" Wall Street shouted.

I turned to see Opera heading back down the sidewalk toward the porch.

"Opera!" I yelled. "Opera, come back!"

But he wasn't coming back.

I looked at Wall Street.

Wall Street looked at me.

We both thought the thoughts the other we thought was thinking, though we didn't think those thoughts were the thoughts we wanted to think.

TRANSLATION:

Like it or not, we had to save our friend.

<small>(I thought.)</small>

So, with a heavy sigh (Don't you just hate dying so early in the morning, it can really ruin your day.), we started after him.

By the time we got to the porch, Opera was already on his second cookie.

"Opera?" I called.

"Munch-munch, crunch-crunch, BURP!" he replied.

"I'm so glad you like them." The old lady smiled. "I saw you hiding in the bushes and thought I'd bake you a quick batch."

"Belch," he belched as he reached for another cookie.

"What about you two?" she asked, holding out the platter to Wall Street and me.

I cleared my throat. "Uh, no, but thanks

anyway." (Mom always taught me to be polite no matter who's trying to poison me.)

"Are you sure?" she asked. "It's been so long since I've cooked for anybody but the Professor."

"Professor?" Wall Street asked.

"Yes, Professor Grimm."

"Is he . . ." I threw a nervous glance up at where the skeleton had been. "Is he able to eat real food? I mean, in his current condition?"

"Whatever do you mean, child?" she asked.

"I mean, that is to say, um, er, ahem . . ." I struggled to find the right words. But how do you tactfully tell a sweet old lady that her house happens to be haunted?

Fortunately, Wall Street saved me the trouble. "He means that creepy ghost you've got living on your roof!" (Good ol' Wall Street.)

But instead of freaking out, the old lady broke into a warm chuckle. "A ghost? Why, what makes you say that, child?"

"'Cause we just saw him," Wall Street said.

"Him?"

"The Professor, the ghost. Outside on the roof."

"Oh my, oh my." Again the woman chuckled. "That wasn't Professor Grimm. That was just one of his inventions."

"Inventions?" I asked.

"Of course." She stepped back and . . .

K-SCREEECH

pushed open the front door.

"Please," she said, smiling, "come inside. I'll be happy to explain it all to you."

She seemed pretty sweet and more than a little frail. No way could she hurt one of us, let alone all three.

I glanced at Opera, who was working on the next to last cookie. He didn't exactly look like he was keeling over from poison.

Maybe she was safe after all.

"Please," she repeated. "Just for a few minutes. Just to keep an old woman company."

I thought of my deal with Wall Street. If there weren't any ghosts in the house, and the old lady could prove it, then for once in my life Wall Street would have to give *me* money.

"Please."

Finally, I nodded and started up the porch steps.

"Wally!" Wall Street cried.

"Relax," I said. "You heard what she said: There are no ghosts here. Just some professor's invention."

"Exactly!" The old woman smiled. Then, offering me the platter, she asked, "Here, would you like the last of the cook—"

Suddenly she was interrupted by a

K-SNATCH
K-CHOMP

and a

"AAAHhh . . ."

Which was definitely not a ghost but the sound of one eataholic beating me to the platter and finishing off the final

BELCH!

cookie.

"Thanks," Opera said. "Those were terrific."

"Don't mention it," she said, laughing. Then turning to me, she added, "But don't you worry. Come inside and I'll whip up another batch."

I nodded and continued toward the door.

"Wally!" Wall Street shouted from the bottom of the porch.

"Come on." I motioned for her to join us.

"No way!"

"Why?" I smirked. "You afraid you were wrong? You afraid you'll discover there are no ghosts?"

"I'm afraid of *becoming* a ghost!"

I turned to the lady. "You'll have to excuse my friend. She's seen one too many horror movies."

"I understand." The little old lady smiled sweetly.

"Wally!"

"You're such a chicken," I said, casually leaning against the boxes piled up near the door.

Well, I wanted to casually lean against them.

Unfortunately, casually leaning usually involves having some coordination. And since coordination isn't exactly my best trait, it was no surprise that the top box slid off the others and crashed to the floor.

This, of course, meant I slid off and joined it on the floor.

Don't worry, it happens all the time.

What does *not* happen all the time is grabbing the next box to pull myself up and pulling it down on top of me.

Even that wasn't a problem, until it broke open and revealed a human corpse.

(Insert "SCREAM!" here.)

A human corpse that was suddenly lying on top of me, its skull and teeth pressed against my face and lips.

(Insert several more **"SCREAMS!"**
along with lots of hysterical
*wheeze, wheeze, wheez*ings
and *gasp, gasp, gasp*ings.)

(Hey, you try staring eyeball-to-eye-socket with a human skull.)

In slightly less time than no time flat, I was on my feet, racing down the porch steps, and screaming for my mommy!

Come to think of it, so were Wall Street and Opera.

(I guess we all have this thing for living.)

We ran down the old lady's walk, threw open the

K-REEEAK . . .
GROOOAAN . . .

gate, and raced home to save our lives (or, in my case, to take a good hot shower—paying particular attention to scrubbing my face and lips).

Chapter 3

Spook Sleuthing

"I'm not sure this is going to solve a thing," I said as I glanced around the public library.

"Don't worry," Wall Street said. "I've seen it in all the detective movies. They always go to libraries and search old newspapers. It's like a tradition or something."

Speaking of traditions . . . I glanced around at all the library shelves towering above us. It would only take one of my world-famous McDoogle trips and falls to crash into the nearest shelf, which would tip over and crash into the next shelf, which would tip over and crash into . . . well, you get the picture. Basically, we're talking about playing Library Shelf Dominoes.

But that was far too predictable for somebody with my experience. No way would I fall for that old cliché . . . particularly with my creative capacity for catastrophes.

So, I just stood there looking over Opera's shoulder as he worked the library's fancy-schmancy computer. As our honorary techno-geek (Opera's the only one who has an iPod surgically wired into his ears.), we figured Opera would know how best to work the thing.

"What are you doing now?" I shouted. (I know shouting's, like, illegal in libraries, but whenever Opera is listening to Rossini or Ravioli or any of those Italian opera guys, he doesn't always hear so well.)

"Professor Grimm!" he shouted back, then took another swig from the diet soda can. (I know it's illegal to bring diet soda into the library, but bribing Opera with food and beverages is the only way to get him to do anything—except when it comes to visiting one of those all-you-can-eat restaurants.)

"Here it is!" he shouted.

Wall Street and I leaned forward to look at the newspaper article. It was dated April 12, 2001, and the headline read:

Local Professor Dies in Auto Accident

That was the bad news.

The badder news was, there was a picture of the guy. A picture that looked exactly like the ghost we'd seen on top of the roof that morning (before he'd lost his clothes and body)!

"Oh, no," I cried.

"Oh, brother," Wall Street groaned.

"Oh, *burp*," Opera burped.

Opera reached for his diet soda and a moment later added another phrase:

"Uh-oh . . ."

This, of course, is the phrase you usually read in G-rated books whenever someone does something incredibly stupid like, oh, I don't know . . . knocking his diet soda can over onto a very expensive library computer!

Of course, there were more sparks and

K-rack, K-sizzle
pop, pop, pop

fireworks than the Fourth of July.

And, of course, I could only stand watching, not because there was a catastrophe, but because for once there was a catastrophe that *I* had not caused.

It was incredible . . . amazing.

In seconds, the entire keyboard was smoking as bad as Dad trying to use the barbecue grill.

I looked for some way to put it out. Unfortunately, there was no fire extinguisher in sight.

Unfortunatelier, the only thing I had to put it out with was a nearby book that I grabbed and used to pat out the flames.

Unfortunateliest, books are made of paper, which you may have noticed have this nasty habit of

K-WHOOSH

catching fire whenever exposed to open flames.

So there I was with a flaming book in my hand trying to

whhh . . . whhh . . . whhh . . .

blow it out.

But my puny breath did no good, so Wall Street

whhh . . . whhh . . . whhh . . .

joined in, which did about the same amount of no good.

Then I had a brainstorm. (All right, with my minor mind it was more like a brain squall . . . actually, a brain-cloudy day.) "Opera!" I cried. "Your soda! Throw the rest of your soda on it!"

Opera looked at me, then at the book, then

at the soda. Finally, he shouted, "No way, I got half a can left!"

(Good ol' Opera.)

By now the entire book was in flames, so I waved it in the air, trying to put it out. Which was a pretty good idea, except for the part of waving it too close to the fire sprinkler in the ceiling. Before I knew it, the alarm

K-RIIIIIIING

sounded, and the sprinkler

K-SWOOOOOSH

went off, gushing water everywhere.

The good news was, the water put out the flames.

The bad news was, it covered the building in half a foot of water, making everyone look like drowned rats and the soaked books look like, well, soaked books.

We turned and sloshed toward the exit as fast as we could.

Of course, I felt bad, but there was a small part of me that was grateful. I mean, if I was destined to destroy the library, at least I did it with some originality.

Unfortunately, I was so impressed with myself that I didn't see the book cart in front of me.

The book cart that I fell onto.

The book cart that rolled through the water until it

*K-Slamm*ed

into the closest bookshelf, which

K-REEEAK
*K-Slamm*ed

into the next bookshelf, which

K-REEEAK . . .

Well, you get the picture. The point is, I wound up playing Library Shelf Dominoes after all—until every shelf in the library was tipped over and floating in water.

Yes sir, old habits can be hard to break.

* * * * *

Of course, they called my folks and made them pay a gazillion dollars for damages. Don't worry, we have a Wally McDoogle Disaster Fund. For a tax-deductible donation just call

1-800-DORK.

We finally made it home (where I'd be grounded until the year 2043). That's when Wall Street called with another idea to make even more money.

Old habits can *really* be hard to break.

"We'll visit a fortune-teller medium, convince her to go to the haunted house, talk to and videotape the ghost, and sell it to cable for—"

"Whoa, whoa, whoa," I interrupted her. "A medium? No way."

"No way, what?"

"No way we're visiting some medium."

"Why not?"

"Our Sunday school teacher says we're not supposed to mess with that stuff."

"Who's messing? We're investigating."

"Forget it," I repeated.

"Great! I'll pick you up, and we'll visit her first thing in the morning."

(Wall Street's never been good at taking no for an answer.)

"Hold it, I just said—"

"See you then!"

CLICK!

(And I've never been good at saying no to disconnected phones.)

So, with nothing else to do, I got ready for bed. Visiting haunted houses is one thing, but visiting mediums . . . well now, that's *a whole other* matter.

So, to help me relax, and drown out the little voice in my head that was quietly whispering:

WARNING! WARNING! WARNING!

I reached for Ol' Betsy and got back to my super-hero story:

```
When we last left Manners Man, he
was sitting down with his family for a
nice turkey dinner.
     "Please pass the mashed potatoes,"
Perfect Daughter, who never pesters
her perfect older brother, says.
     "Why, certainly, dear," Perfect
Mom, who never raises her perfect
voice, replies.
     "Yeah, Miss Piggy," her brother says,
"go ahead and chow down."
```

Perfect Daughter looks up in surprise. "Pardon me?"

"If you get any fatter they'll have to use two ZIP codes to get you your mail delivered."

Perfect Daughter blinks in surprise. "I'm sorry, I don't understand."

"You don't understand? Well, maybe this will help." Immediately her brother pushes up his nose and starts, "Oink-oink, oink-oink-oink"ing!

Manners Man drops his fork in surprise. "Excuse me? What are you doing, young man?"

"Just having a conversation with my favorite piglet," her brother sneers between his oinking.

"That'll be enough of that!" Perfect Mom replies.

But her son continues snorting and oinking until his little sister begins to cry.

"Why are you doing this to me?" she sobs. "I don't understand," says Perfect Daughter who helplessly turns to Perfect Mom. "Oh, Mother, why is he tormenting me so?"

"Shut yer mouth!" Mom snaps. "And

quit crying before I really give you something to cry about."

"Yeah," her brother says, laughing, "like no dessert."

"What is happening here?" Manners Man demands.

To which Perfect Daughter turns on him and sneers, "Maybe if you'd use your head for something other than a hatrack, you'd figure it out."

Manners Man politely gasps. "You... you're all becoming extremely rude."

"You think?" Mom taunts.

"He thinks?" His son laughs. "Since when?"

Putting all the pieces together, Manners Man concludes, "This must be the work of that diabolically dubious and dangerous...

(Ta-da-Daaaa...)

Rude Dude!"

"Hey, everybody," Perfect Wife sneers and says, "give Einstein here a cigar."

Unable to put up with any more rudeness, our hero leaps from the

table—but only after asking to be
excused and complimenting his wife for
preparing such an excellent meal.

"Yeah, whatever..."

He then races to his office and
speaks into the voice-activated wall:
"Excuse me, please. If it's not too
much bother, I would appreciate your
opening the secret panel for me."

Immediately the wall slides open,
revealing the secret entrance to Manners
Cave.

After politely thanking the wall,
Manners Man leaps onto the pole and
slides down to his cave, where he quickly
activates his Manners Computer—dialing
dials, switching switches, and knobbing
knobs.

Soon the voice-activated computer
replies, "Good evening, kind sir."

"Good evening, Computer. Listen, I
need you to—"

"How was your dinner?"

"Fine. Listen, I need you to—"

"I trust your turkey was cooked to
perfec—"

"Will you shut up and listen to
me!" Instantly, Manners Man throws his

hands over his mouth. "Oh, no, it is happening to me as well! Please, please, forgive me."

"Certainly."

Exercising all of his strength and self-control, our hero says, "Show me the latest location of Rude Dude."

To his surprise, the computer does not answer.

"Computer?"

"Yes."

"Show me the latest information on Rude Dude!"

Again, there is no answer.

"Computer, what's wrong?"

"I'm waiting for the magic word."

"Magic word? Magic word?! The fate of the entire civilized world hangs in the balance, and you're waiting for a magic word?!!"

"Yes, if it is not too terribly inconvenient."

Fighting the urge to shout back a hundred sarcastic sayings, our superhero racks his mind until he has it:

"PLEASE! Please show me the hideout of Rude Dude."

"It would be my pleasure."

A faint image flickers on the screen as the computer politely asks, "And?"

"And...uh, uh, and thank you! Thank you very much!"

"You're very welcome, it has been my pleasure."

The image appears, and our hero clearly sees Rude Dude's hideout. But there is absolutely no sign of the creepily crude communicator. There is...

—No cell phone that he rudely lets ring in the middle of movies.
—No video game that he rudely plays too loud.
—Not even any dirty socks that he rudely leaves for his mom to pick up.

"This is incredibly lame!" Manners Man cries. "If I can't find that jerk, I can't stop his rudeness from spreading. And if I can't stop it from spreading—"

"Wally?" Mom called from the bottom of the stairs. "Are you in bed?"

I looked up from Ol' Betsy. "Yes, Mom, I'm sound asleep." I've never been very good at lying (and I hope I never get the hang of it).

"You turn off that computer now and get some sleep. It's way past your bedtime."

Reluctantly, I shut Ol' Betsy down. It looked like I'd have to wait until after we visited the medium before I could continue the story . . . provided they let you take laptops to heaven.

Chapter 4

Busting Ghost Business

Wall Street reached over and gave another

knock-knock-knock

on the door—which is not to be confused with the

*KNOCK-KNOCK-KNOCK*ing

of my knees or the

*CHATTER, CHATTER, CHATTER*ing

of my teeth. It's not that I was scared—I always break out into a good case of *knock*ing and *chatter*ing every time I'm about to die.

I stood with Opera, pretending to be calm and collected. But it's hard to be calm and collected when you're in the middle of something you're not supposed to be doing. Especially if that something involves standing in front of a fortune-teller's shop with a giant palm painted on the window that has all sorts of wizard hats, magic wands, magic potions, crystal balls, and, of course, a three-for-one sale on Pairy Hotter books.

"Don't look so worried," Opera said as he dug into his third bag of Chippy Chipper potato chips. (Hey, it was already 9:03 a.m., a guy's got to snack on something between those in-between-meal snacks.) He continued, "Ninety-nine percent of all mediums and fortune-tellers are fake."

I relaxed slightly. "And the other 1 percent?" I asked.

"They're either possessed by evil spirits or working in league with the devil."

y,"

a

k

"O   I said, my voice rising two and a half octaves as I turned and started down the street. But I'd barely taken a step before the door

K-REEEAKed

open and an old woman with long gray hair

peered out at us. I don't want to say she was
ugly, but picture the Wicked Witch of the West
BEFORE she had her beauty makeover.

"May I help you?" Her voice *creaked* louder
than the door.

"Are you Madame Mystic?" Wall Street asked.

"Yes."

"We've come for the free trial."

"Oh, yes, why, certainly. Do come in." She
opened the door wider.

It

*K-REEEAK*ed

louder.

I prayed harder.

Opera and Wall Street stepped inside.

I, of course, tried stepping farther outside
(like running down the street and screaming for
my life all the way home).

But there's something about being dragged
in kicking and screaming by your two best
friends that can make escaping with your life a
little difficult.

We entered the first room. It was full of
shelves with jars and jars of weird stuff for sale.

"What's this?" Wall Street asked, picking up
the closest jar.

"Be careful!" Madame Mystic warned. She snatched it from Wall Street's hands and carefully put it back on the shelf.

"Why, it's just dirt!"

"But it's very special dirt. It has been trod upon by Valkamore himself—the king of the invisible vampires."

"Invisible vampires?" Wall Street said scornfully. "There's no such thing as invisible vampires."

"Why do you say that?" the woman asked.

"Nobody's ever seen them."

"Then they're doing a very good job, wouldn't you agree?"

Wall Street glanced at me and rolled her eyes so hard I thought she'd sprain them.

"Would you like to buy some of the dirt?" the old woman asked. "I could make you a real deal."

"How much?" Opera asked.

"For the entire jar—just $499.95, plus shipping and handling."

Wall Street and I traded looks. We both knew what the other was thinking. When it comes to making money off suckers, maybe Wall Street was in the wrong business.

"What about this?" Opera asked, reaching for a jar that was completely empty.

"Ah." Madame Mystic smiled. "My treasured Ghost Breath."

"Ghost Breath?" he said, peering inside. "It looks like ordinary air."

"But it isn't," she said.

"Why, what's the difference?"

"The difference is, this air costs $749.95 a jar."

Opera opened his mouth, then stopped and nodded in complete understanding. (When it comes to ghosts, he's never been the brightest candle on the cake.)

"Wait a minute," Wall Street argued. "Ghosts are dead. They don't breathe."

"Exactly." The old woman nodded.

"So how can this be Ghost Breath if ghosts don't breathe?"

"That's why this air is so rare and expensive," Madame Mystic said.

"Oh, brother," I muttered as I passed by Opera, who was still examining the jar.

"Oh, sister," Wall Street mumbled as she joined me at the other end of the room.

"Do you take credit cards?" Opera asked as he reached for his billfold.

Eventually, we passed through a curtain of colored beads and entered a room darker than the circles under Mom's eyes when she's been up all night taking care of me when I'm sick.

In the center was a table with four chairs around it. On top of the table was a glass bowl.

"What's that?" Wall Street asked.

"A salad bowl, for seeing spirits."

"A salad bowl," I scoffed. "Aren't you supposed to have, like, a crystal ball for seeing stuff like that?"

The old woman shrugged. "Crystal balls are expensive, and I'm on a fixed income. Besides, salad bowls bring in the vegetarian ghosts and those wanting to watch their weight. Now, please have a seat."

* * * * *

Five minutes later we sat in the dark, holding hands around a table covered with a paper tablecloth. (I guess real tablecloths are expensive, too.)

Madame Mystic's eyes were closed as she rolled her head from side to side. "Yes . . . ," she moaned. "I sense the presence of a spirit from beyond."

Opera sat to my right, so scared that he actually stopped cramming chips into his mouth. Of course, he was still chewing—he had enough stored in his cheeks to last a week, in case of emergencies.

Wall Street sat across from me. She believed in ghosts, but this was obviously a scam.

And me. Well, I knew that the woman was a fake. But the dark, creepy room was, oh, I don't know . . . kind of dark and creepy.

"Yes . . . ," Madame Mystic groaned, "a spirit from beyond the grave has chosen to visit us."

I shifted uneasily in my chair.

Opera stopped chewing.

Another voice suddenly

$$oooOOo_{ooo}oo OOO_{ooOoo} . . .$$

filled the air.

I glanced nervously at Wall Street.

"CD player," she whispered. "Remote control."

I glanced at Madame Mystic. It must be pretty hard operating a remote when she was holding our hands.

"Her feet," Wall Street explained. "She's doing it with her feet."

Madame Mystic's eyes were still closed, so I ducked under the table to take a peek.

So did Wall Street.

We saw the same thing . . .

Nothing. No switches, no hidden remotes. Nothing.

I glanced back at Wall Street. She didn't look quite as confident. She grew even less confident when an icy wind swept down onto the table.

Again, we checked her hands.

Again, we checked her feet.

And again, we saw . . .

Nothing.

Madame Mystic said, "I see the face of an old man." With eyes still closed, she turned to Opera. "It is your father come back to join us from the dead."

"Actually," Opera said, clearing his throat, "my father is alive and works at the paper mill."

"Right." The woman nodded. "Of course, I meant your grandfather."

"Uh, no, he's alive, too."

"Did I say your grandfather? Actually, it's your grandfather's father's father's father."

"Yes!" Opera nodded enthusiastically. "He *is* dead! How did you know?"

"The spirits have told me."

Opera leaned over to me and whispered, "Is she good or what?!"

I was still hoping for "or what," but my hopes faded when I suddenly heard the sound of a shaking tambourine.

I glanced at Wall Street. By now the wind was so strong, her hair was blowing all over the place. But I could still see her eyes. They grew as big as saucers.

And for good reason.

I looked over my shoulder just in time to see the tambourine flying at me!

I ducked as it sailed over my head. Then it slowed and hovered above the table

*shake, shake, shak*ing
and
*clang, clang, clang*ing

away. I took an unsteady breath, telling myself not to be scared.

Unfortunately, *myself* wasn't exactly in the mood for listening. To be honest, it felt a lot more like jumping up, screaming hysterically, and running out of there.

Several seconds passed (or lifetimes, if you count how fast my heart was beating). Finally, the tambourine moved off, floating out of the room—still *shak*ing and *clang*ing.

Yes sir, on the Let's Weird Wally Out Scale of 1 to 10, we were pushing a 12.

But apparently the fun and games still weren't quite over.

When I looked back at Wall Street, her eyes were no longer the size of saucers. Now they were more like dinner plates, then satellite dishes, then trampolines, then—well, you get the point.

With dread, I looked back over my shoulder.

The good news was, it wasn't a shaking tambourine coming at me.

The bad news was, it was a burning candelabra! With a dozen flaming candles smoking and sputtering!

Call me a spoilsport, but as much as I wanted to stick around and have a few more heart attacks, or at least a good healthy

"AUGHHHH!"

(That, of course, was the world-famous
McDoogle scream, followed quickly by
a
K-Thud!
. . . the world-famous McDoogle faint),

I told myself it was best to leap up and run for all I was worth.

Unfortunately, this time I listened to myself.

It wasn't unfortunate that I leaped up.

It *was* unfortunate that my head

*K-Lunk*ed

into the floating candelabra.

Even that wouldn't have been so bad, if the little collision hadn't sent the big thing . . .

*K-Crash*ing

to the table, where it immediately

*K-whoosh*ed

the paper tablecloth on fire, lighting up the entire room and exposing a black rope hanging down from the ceiling.

A black rope that had been invisible until then.

A black rope that immediately caught fire from the burning tablecloth.

A black rope that quickly burned all the way up to the ceiling.

Then things started to get interesting. . . .

By now Madame Mystic was screaming, "What are you doing?! What are you doing?!"

(The poor thing had obviously not read any of these books, or she would have known I was simply having another one of my world-famous, patent-pending *McDoogle Mishaps*.)

But everybody else knew, which explained their jumping to their feet and yelling in hysteria.

It would also explain the ceiling above the table catching fire from the rope.

It would even explain the new voice that suddenly cried from above our heads: . . .

"YEOOOOW!"

We all looked up.

So did Madame Mystic. "My," she shouted, "the spirits are active today!"

"OUCH! OUCH! OUCH!"

Madame Mystic shouted louder, "Maybe they should be a little less active!"

The voice cried even louder:

"OUCH! OUCH! OUCH!"

"I SAID, MAYBE THE SPIRITS SHOULD BE A LITTLE LESS—"

But that's as far as she got before the burning ceiling collapsed and

*K-SMASH*ed

onto the table.

But not just the ceiling . . .

There were also a few gizmos, like:

—a CD boom box still playing

"*. . . oooOOOooooo . . .*"

—a giant electric fan still blowing cold air

—and a tambourine still attached to a
   different black rope.

Oh, yeah, and there was one other thing. . . .

A man dressed in black, who had obviously
been running those gizmos!

"Bernard!" Madame Mystic rushed to him.
"Bernard, are you all right?"

"I'm fine, Mom," the young man groaned.
"Just . . . fine."

Of course, we didn't stick around and give a
second opinion. If the man was fine, then we
were . . .

Gone!

But not before leaving them an address to
send the bill for all the damages.

(Dad was going to love this one.)

Chapter 5

A Family Meal

That night, as my family ate dinner (Well, tried to eat—since it was my little sister Carrie's turn to cook.), I thought I would try a little good old-fashioned, family discussion.

"So . . . ," I said, pushing the mashed potatoes around on my plate so it would look like I'd actually taken a bite. (I *did* say it was my sister's turn to cook, right?)

I continued, "I know this guy who knows this guy who claims he, like, saw a ghost!"

I waited for a response. There was nothing but the usual

> *K-runch, K-runch*
> *K-rackle, K-rackle*
> "Ow! I think I broke a tooth!"

that comes whenever we eat Carrie's mashed potatoes.

I tried again, this time turning to my dad. "So tell me, Dad, what do you think about that?"

He looked up, startled. "Huh? What? How much is it going to cost me?"

"It doesn't cost anything."

"Then, sure, go ahead, why not."

"Herb?" Mom frowned.

Again he looked up. "What? Oh, right. Better check with your mother first."

Good ol' Dad. The guy was obviously flying on autoparent.

I turned to my older twin brothers, Burt and Brock. "What do you guys think?"

But Burt (Or was it Brock? I get them mixed up.) was too busy stuffing his mashed potatoes into a napkin to hide them.

And Brock (Or was it Burt?) was too busy slipping them off his plate and down to our cat, Collision—which would explain the

"MREOOOW!"
cough, cough, gag, gag

that our cat makes whenever she goes into convulsions from eating Carrie's food.

That left only Carrie and Mom.

I would have asked Carrie, but she was too

busy passing around seconds and thirds to my brothers . . . who were busily borrowing napkins.

So that left Mom.

"What do you think?" I asked her.

"About ghosts and the supernatural?"

"Yeah?"

"I don't believe in ghosts," she said.

"Why not?"

"The Bible says that when we die we go to face God."

"Meaning?"

"Meaning we don't stop off and haunt houses or make special guest appearances at séances along the way."

"But you believe in the supernatural?" I asked.

"Like demons and angels? Absolutely," she said.

"Because?"

"Because the Bible talks about them."

I nodded.

She continued, "But, Wally, I also believe we shouldn't mess with some of those things." Turning to Carrie, she asked, "Sweetheart, could I have more of those delicious nuts?"

Carrie frowned. "Nuts? I didn't fix any nuts."

"Oh. . . . Well, whatever those hard little crunchy things are."

"You mean the peas?"

"Those are peas?"

"Yeah." Carrie grinned sheepishly. "I may have fried them a bit too long."

Mom's jaw dropped. "You fried the—" Then, catching herself, she cranked up a smile. "Well, they're the best fried peas I've ever had, sweetheart." She then proceeded to

K-rattle-rattle-rattle

dump several spoonfuls of the gravel-like peas onto her plate.

"Why do you say that?" I asked.

"Because I'm her mother, and I'm supposed to praise her cooking."

"No, no," I said. "I mean, why aren't we supposed to mess with that stuff?"

"Because it's the occult and it's dangerous."

"*Occult?*" I asked.

"Like witches, wizards, mediums, and that sort of thing." She began spreading the peas around her plate, trying to hide them under her mashed potatoes.

"How is that dangerous?"

"I'm not entirely sure," she said. "But you might want to ask Simon Figledoober. I know he was involved in that stuff a long time ago."

"Mr. Figledoober, the pet-store owner?"

"That's right." She looked down at her plate. There was still a small pile of peas visible. "Wally," she asked, "may I borrow your napkin for a minute?"

"Sure," I said as I handed it to her.

"Thanks." She grinned gratefully.

* * * * *

That night as I climbed into bed, I was still pretty stressed, so I grabbed Ol' Betsy and went to work:

When we last left our reasonably reliable and really responsible Manners Man, he was searching in vain for the one and only——(although at the moment there doesn't appear to be a one, let alone an only)——

(Insert bad-guy music here.)

Rude Dude.

It seems the repugnant and riotously ribald Rude Dude (Can you believe those words are actually in the dictionary?)

is spreading his rudeness everywhere.
Even our hero is getting a little, how
shall we put it, impolite.

"Oh, shut up. I am not."

(See what I mean?)

"Listen, Mr. Author, let's see you
try battling the World's Most Malicious
Menace to Manners when you can't even
find where to battle him."

(I just hate it when make-believe
characters talk back, don't you?)

I reach for Ol' Betsy's keys and type my
answer. "Maybe if you were to ask me politely, I
would tell you."

"Maybe if you were to tell the story
like a halfway normal author with half
a brain, I'd find him," he says.

"Well, at least I have a brain," I type. "All
you are is a bunch of letters on this page."

"Oh, yeah? Well, all you are is some
clueless kid afraid of ghosts!"

"Well, all you are is a character I'm about to
DELETE!"

"Well, all you are is—" Suddenly, he stops. "Great garbanzo beans," he shouts, "it's happening even to us!"

I type, "What is, you respectless runt?"

"That!"

"That what?"

"That rudeness."

I look up from Ol' Betsy. He was right! Quickly, I type, "So what do we do?"

"You're the author, brainless boy, you tell me."

"You're the superjerk superhero, you tell me."

"You're the—"

Suddenly, I type, "IT'S HAPPENING AGAIN!"

Our superhero grabs his superhead and gives it a supershake. "Yes. Yes. It's so sneaky the way it creeps up on us."

"We have to be ultracareful."

"And ultrapolite."

I nod.

"So where do we go from here?" he asks.

"Do you mind if I put you outside on the street to start tracking down Rude Dude?"

"That would be a swell idea, and thanks for asking, you mindless moron of mediocrity—AUGH! I'm sorry, I'm sorry."

"That's okay," I type as I go back to work. . . .

Suddenly, our superhero streaks speedily to the streets searching for the sinisterly suspicious suspect—

(Insert more bad-guy music here.)

"You've already done that, you brainless, er, uh, brainy boy of beautiful books."

"Why, yes, I have," I type. "Thank you so much."

"You're certainly welcome."

Suddenly, our superhero strides the streets searching for the supersarcastic speaker of snide snippets...Rude Dude.

He flags down a bus, which slows to a stop and opens its doors. Then, just before he steps on board, the bus speeds up.

The driver lets out a rude

"Moo-hoo-hoo-ha-ha-ha!"

laugh and stops the bus ten feet away.

Manners Man races to get on board, only to have the bus start off again.

"Excuse me," our hero asks, "what are you doing?"

"Just having some fun," the driver shouts as he stops another ten feet away.

Once again our hero races toward the bus, and once again it pulls away.

"I don't understand your behavior!" Manners Man shouts.

"He's just being rude," I type. "May I suggest calling for a taxi?"

"What about all my superhero super-stuff?"

"I'm saving that for the next section."

Our hero nods as he spins around to an approaching taxi. "Oh, taxi," he shouts. "If you don't mind, I would greatly appreciate your stopping so that I—"

K-Bamb!

That, of course, is the sound of a taxicab crashing into a superhero and sending him sailing into the air.

I smiled as I reached for the keyboard and typed, "That'll teach you for calling me a 'mindless moron of mediocrity.'"

All right, I'll admit it was a little rude. Okay, okay, a lot rude. But I always get rude when I get stressed. And who wouldn't be stressed with all that has been happening: ghosts, fortune-tellers, séances. And now I am getting ready to visit some guy who has been involved with the occult.

With a heavy sigh, I reach down and type a quick note to Manners Man:

"Sorry about the taxi. I'll fix things when I get back from my meeting with Mr. Figledoober."

o,"
s

e
p
o
h

e
r
u
s

"I

Manners
Man
shouts.

"Why's that?" I type.

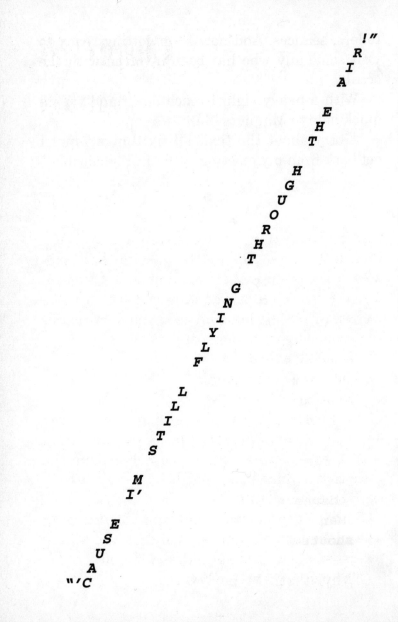

"'Cause I'm still flying through the air!"

Chapter 6

Truth or Scare

Early the next morning I stepped into Mr. Figledoober's pet shop. After all that had happened, I was still pretty nervous and a lot confused. I glanced around and was glad that there were no floating tambourines, candelabras, or spooky ghosts with long, pointy fingers.

"Hello?" I called.

There was no answer.

"Hello. . . ."

Still nothing in the answer department. And for good reason. There was nobody there. Not a soul. It was just me, my frayed nerves, and the voice that suddenly screamed.

"It's about time!"

The good news was, nothing was burning when I leaped out of my skin and hit the ceiling (which meant no fire sprinklers went off).

The bad news was, when I . . .

*K-Thudd*ed

back to the floor and regained consciousness, there was still nobody in the shop.

At least nobody who was visible.

At least nobody who had a body.

I rose nervously to my feet.

Mom had said Mr. Figledoober had been involved with junk like the occult and spirits. As I looked around the shop, I hoped she'd used the right word when she said "had."

"S-s-sorry I'm late," I said, searching the store for somebody. For anybody. But the place was more deserted than the kitchen when Mom's looking for somebody to do dishes.

Suddenly, the voice yelled from behind me, "It's about time!"

I gasped and spun around.

There was still nobody there.

At least nobody mortal.

After saying a few dozen prayers, I decided it was time to step forward and be a man. I took a deep breath and shouted in my most courageous voice:

"I w-w-w-want my m-m-m-m-mommy!"

(Well, all right, maybe that wasn't so courageous, but at least it got an answer.)

"Have a seat!"

Being a polite guest, I immediately dropped to the floor and sat. (I'm guessing ghosts hate it when you have bad manners.)

But for some reason he wasn't satisfied. He had drifted to my left and shouted:

"Have a seat!"

I figured he wasn't crazy about me sitting on his floor, so I got up and looked for a chair.

"Have a seat!"

I dropped back to the floor. Now he was to my right, as invisible (and mad) as ever.

"Have a seat!"

I figured he didn't like the way I was sitting. So, I sat up straighter and crossed my legs.

"H-h-how's this?" I asked.

"It's about time!"

"S-s-sorry."

"Have a seat!"

"Pardon me? I am sit—"

"Have a seat! Have a seat!"

I frowned. Maybe some ghosts are hard of hearing. Or seeing. Or maybe when they get old they start forgetting, like Grandpa. I cleared my voice and shouted louder, "Excuse me, but I *am* sitting and—"

"Wally?"

Oh, great, there was another one coming at me from the other side of the room.

"It's about time!" The first voice cried.

"Wally?" The second voice was moving. Getting closer.

I was cowering, getting more nervous.

"Wally?"

Finally, I managed to squeak out a little "Present!"

"What on earth—"

I lifted my eyes to see Mr. Figledoober standing at the end of the aisle with his hands on his hips. "What are you doing on the floor?"

"Have a seat!" the other voice commanded. "Have a seat!"

I motioned to the voice, and Mr. Figledoober broke out laughing. "That's just Barnabas."

"What-abas?" I croaked.

He turned and called. "Barnabas, come here. Have a seat."

Immediately a green parrot flew across the store and landed on Mr. Figledoober's shoulder.

"Have a seat! Have a seat!" Barnabas cawed as Mr. Figledoober reached into his sweater pocket for a handful of sunflower seeds.

He pulled them out and opened his palm as the bird squawked, "It's about time! It's about time!" while gobbling them down.

* * * * *

Of course, we all had a good laugh—at least Mr. Figledoober and Barnabas did. I was too busy thanking God that I hadn't become ghost toast.

"So," Mr. Figledoober said as we approached a cage full of hamsters (which I'm more than a little allergic to), "your mother said you have some questions about the occult."

I nodded, feeling my nose beginning to tickle.

He motioned for me to sit down on a desk chair with wheels while he sat up on the counter. "Fire away. Ask me anything you like."

"Mom says you were involved in that stuff."

"Yes, I'm sorry to say that I was."

"Why are you sorry?"

"Because it's dangerous."

"That's what everybody says. But why is it da—" I felt a sneeze coming on and shoved my finger under my nose.

"Why is it dangerous?" he asked.

Keeping my finger in place, I nodded.

"For two reasons," he said. "The first is because most of it is just silly superstition."

I took my finger away from my nose to ask, "Why are—

"Ahh . . ."

and quickly shoved it back under again.

"Why are superstitions dangerous?" he asked for me. I nodded.

"Superstitions control people. We start doing things out of fear. We're no longer doing what we want, but what the superstition tells us we're supposed to do."

Again I tried to speak. "Even though it's silly an—

"Ahh . . ."

I grabbed my nose and again he spoke for me. "Even though it's silly and not real?"

I nodded, wanting to sneeze so bad my eyes began to water.

"That's right."

I tried again. "What about witches, mediums, an—

"Ahh, ahhhh . . ."

"Witches, mediums, and all that?"

I nodded.

"A lot of kids dabble in that stuff because they think it's cool or because they hope it will give them control of their life. But often what happens is they become controlled by the superstitions. If they're lucky."

"If they—

"Ahh, ahhhh, ahhhhhh . . ."

I grabbed my nose, feeling like I was about to explode.

He nodded. "That's where the second danger comes in. Because once in a while the stuff is real. And when that happens, it's very dangerous."

"Why's tha—

"Ahh, ahhhh, ahhhhhh, ahhhhhhhh . . ."

"Because then you're messin' with the devil, and he's only got one thing in mind."

I looked at him and waited for him to speak.

He continued. "He wants to control or destroy you."

I gulped nervously—still holding my nose, with my eyes watering worse than when our toilet backs up.

"That's why the Bible clearly warns us to stay away from all that."

I wanted to ask him where it said that, but by now tears were streaming down my cheeks.

As if reading my mind, he quietly quoted: "'*Do not go to mediums or fortune-tellers for advice.*' Leviticus 19:31."

I sat there for a long moment, thinking over what he had said. I had my answer. The guy definitely knew what he was talking about. Satisfied, I took a deep breath and blew it out.

Unfortunately, this meant letting go of my nose.

Unfortunatelier, this meant letting go of the biggest

"AH-CHOOOOOOOOOOOOO!!!"

in recorded history.

Of course, I felt really bad for drenching Mr. Figledoober. But I had little time to apologize 'cause the sneeze shot me (and my chair) backward.

We rolled across the pet shop like a rocket car on caffeine.

Fortunately, rocket cars have brakes and parachutes to stop them.

Unfortunately, all I had was a

K-RASH!
K-WHOOSH!
glug, glug, glug

fishtank, with plenty of fish

*Flap, flap, flapp*ing

all over me.

"Wally!" Mr. Figledoober raced to my side. "Wally, are you all right?"

After lots of

*Cough, cough, cough*ing,
*Gag, gag, gagg*ing,

and the usual

*Drown, drown, drown*ing,

I finally opened my mouth and managed to gasp: "Better phone Dad and tell him another bill is on the way."

Chapter 7

Stake Out!

I was feeling pretty bad about leaving Manners Man sailing through the air. So, as soon as I got home from the pet shop, I dried off, pulled a couple more goldfish from my underwear, and went back to work:

When we last left our highflying hero, he was flying higher than any highflying hero should ever have to fly.

That's the bad news.

The good news is, he is flying so high that he

K-Rashes

through the window of a seventy-eight-story building.

"That's good news?" he asks his author.

"Trust me," I write.

After pulling chunks of broken glass out of his hair and body—

"Ouch! Ouch!"
"Ooooch! Ooooch!"

"You're sure this is good news?!"

"Absolutely," I said and started again.

After pulling chunks of broken glass out of his hair and various body parts, and setting a few broken bones along the way—
"Oh, yeah, that's great news!"

"Please, Manners Man."

"That's my name, don't wear it out."

"Oh, brother, you're being rude again."

"I'm so terribly sorry." He sighs.

"Was that sarcasm?" I ask.

"No, I was being sincere."

I nod and start once again.

After pulling out the glass and resetting his bones, he notices he's landed in a hospital room. But not just any hospital room. Oh, no, dear reader, that would be way too boring. Instead, because of some very clever writing on this author's part, he's landed in the hospital room of...

Ta-da-Daaaa...

"Wait a minute," Manners Man complains. "That's bad-guy music again."

I nod and continue.

"Because he's landed in the very room of

Ta-da-Daaaa...

Rude Dude!"

"Cool!" our hero shouts.

"Thanks," our writer writes.

Manners Man spins around and sees the baddest of bad boys lying in bed wearing a cast. But not just a cast on his arms or legs or neck parts. No way. Instead, it's a cast on his every part.

"Rude Dude. What are you doing here?" he shouts.

"Muff mwa mooble ma," the monstrously mean man mumbles.

Realizing "every part" also means his mouth part, our hero quickly rushes to Rude Dude and shatters the cast around his mouth.

Now the dude rudely answers, "Thanks, Moron Man."

"Please, there's no need to be rude."

"I can't help it," the bad boy explains. "It's in my contract. If I'm not rude, they'll give my job to someone else."

"That's terrible."

"Tell me about it, you pathetic pinhead of a person."

Trying to overlook the insult, our hero repeats, "How did you get here?"

"My assistant did this! That creepy robot is trying to takeover the world with his own brand of rudeness."

"A robot did this?"

"A remote-controlled roving robot referred to as Rudy."

"A remote-controlled roving robot referred to as Rudy is the reason for the rudeness?"

"A remote-controlled roving robot referred to as Rudy is the reason for the rudeness unreasonably rampaging our region."

"Wow, you're good with those tongue twisters," our hero says.

"Yeah." Rude Dude smirks. "See if you can top that."

Manners Man takes a deep breath and gives it his best shot... "A remote-controlled roving robot referred to as Rudy is the reason for the rudeness unreasonably rampaging our region regardless of the rational reasons researched in recalling references to Rudy's unreasonableness."

"Yikes!" Rude Dude exclaims. "No wonder you're the superhero of this story."

"Thank you," Manners Man replies.

"So how do we stop him?" Rude Dude asks.

"Where is he?"

"He's in a submarine broadcasting signals that take over everyone's brains and make them incredibly rude!"

"You mean like those TV shows from Hollywood?"

"Worse!"

"Worse?! Then we must combine forces to stop him!"

"But how?"

"Don't worry," Manners Man says. "I'll just, uh——" He looks down at his gizmo belt. But alas and alack (whatever that means), it's nowhere to be found.

"Excuse me, Mr. Writer, didn't you say I'd have cool superhero stuff in this section?"

"Sorry," I type. "It slipped my mind. But hang on . . ."

Suddenly, a nurse throws open the door. In her hands is a superhero gizmo belt.

"I found this superhero gizmo belt outside," she rudely says. "Which of you two losers does it belong to?"

"That, uh"—our hero raises his hand—"that would be me."

Without a word, she dumps it on the floor and storms off. Immediately, our hero races to it and looks for just the right superhero gizmo.

"Let's see here, we have...

—jet-powered roller skates,
—a turbocharged can opener,
—exploding chewing gum...

Ah, here we go."

He pulls out his Chain Saw Cast Cutter (sold at superhero stores everywhere) and immediately

rev...rev...revs

it up. He then

rip...rip...rips

through the cast and frees Rude Dude.
  Together they turn and

K-RASH!
"AUGHhhhhhh..."

leap out the window.
  Then, just before they hit, Rude
Dude turns to our hero. "Excuse me,
Mindless Man, how exactly will we
avoid smashing our superselves onto
that superhard superhighway below us?"
  "Relax," our hero says, chuckling,
"I'll just reach down to my superhero
gizmo belt and, uh, um, er..."
  "You left it in the room, didn't
you?"
  "Well, um, uh, um, er..."
  Great granola bars! What will happen
next? How will our superfellows stop
from becoming superhighway smudges?
How will they rein in Rudy the remote-
controlled robot's rudeness?
  These and other questions haunt
their hollow heads...
  "We heard that!"

  "Sorry."

These and other questions haunt their handsome heads, when suddenly—

Wall Street's special tone rings on my cell phone.

$$\text{\$\$\$ I want your money! \$\$\$}$$
$$\text{\$\$\$ I want your money! \$\$\$}$$

With apologies to Rude Dude and Manners Man, I turned from Ol' Betsy, picked up the phone, and answered. "Hello."

"I got great news, Wally." (Of course, great news to Wall Street means great poverty to me.) "I've rented all sorts of cool ghost-detection stuff."

"What do we need ghost-detection stuff for?"

"To detect the ghosts," she said.

I felt my mouth going dry. "What ghosts?"

"The ones we'll see when we break into the haunted house tonight."

I tried to answer, but my heart had already leaped up into my throat.

"Relax," she said. "We're not going inside by ourselves."

"We're not?"

"Of course not. I've talked Madame Mystic, that old fortune-teller, into coming with us."

"But you don't believe in her?"

"No, but she has the best and only ghost-detecting stuff in town," Wall Street said.

"Oh, no . . . ," I groaned.

"Oh, yes . . . ," she exclaimed.

* * * * *

I don't know how she did it, but somehow Wall Street (a.k.a. Queen of the Fast Talkers) got us all there . . . and with toys!

—Opera, had his Ghost Detector Radar Dish . . . (which could have been passed off as any ordinary home satellite dish).
—Wall Street, had her Ghost Detector DVD Recorder . . . (which could have been passed off as any ordinary home recorder).
—And yours truly, had my Ghost Detector Knocking Knees . . . (which could have been passed off as any ordinary time I'm about to die).

Oh, yeah, and then there was Madame Mystic, our fortune-teller friend. She gave us a real deal on all the ghost-detecting equipment—just $99 a month for ninety-nine years—which seemed expensive until she saw our futures and claimed we'd make a gazillion dollars using the stuff.

(Hey, if you can't trust a fake fortune-teller, who can you trust?)

Of course, I still had a major problem with her. (Believe it or not, I didn't forget what Mr. Figledoober had said.) And, as we approached the house, I whispered to Wall Street, "Why's she here?"

"She comes with the equipment," Wall Street explained. "Besides, she's an expert."

"An expert fake," I answered.

"Exactly." Wall Street beamed. "As an expert fake, she's an expert at detecting fake experts."

Opera stepped in. "But if she's an expert fake, how do we know she's not faking being an expert fake detecting fake experts?"

Wall Street shrugged. "How do we know she's not faking being an expert fake who's not faking being an expert fake detecting fake—"

"Guys!" I interrupted.

They looked at me.

"I just finished a bunch of double-talk about a robot in my superhero story. Can we do something else?"

Opera shrugged. "If you say so."

Wall Street nodded. "I'll say so if you say so."

Opera shrugged again. "I'll say so if you say so, since Wally said—"

"GUYS!"

"Sorry." (They said so.)

We had just arrived at a house across the street from the Professor's when suddenly the porch light went on.

"Get down!" Wall Street whispered.

We dropped to our knees and crawled to the closest bunch of bushes.

I poked my head out from under a branch to take a peek. The old housekeeper was

K-reeeak

opening the door. In her hands was a black cat. With a soft groan, she stooped over and set the animal outside.

"There you go, Balzac," she said. "I'll see you in the morning, dear."

Then she turned, stepped back into the house, and

K-reeeak

shut the door.

We watched and waited.

Then we waited and watched.

Suddenly, shadows darted across the house, across the yard, across everywhere!

"What's that?!" I whispered.

Madame Mystic nodded toward the sky. "Just clouds."

We looked up to see dark, black clouds shooting across the full moon.

"It's perfectly natural," she said with confidence. "Everything has a natural explanation."

It was nice to know she was finally being honest with us. We nodded in agreement and turned back to the house.

"What do we do now?" I asked.

"Just wait till she goes to bed," Wall Street explained.

"And then what?"

"And then we go inside."

"We *what*?!" I cried.

"Relax," Wall Street said. "There's no way that old housekeeper would show us around the house, let alone tell us the truth. Remember, she said Professor Grimm is still alive when he isn't."

"So?"

"So we'll have to search the place for ourselves."

I coughed and let out a mighty "*Squeak!*"

I cleared my voice and tried again. "*Croak!*"

I tried one last time and managed to get out a "H-h-how?!"

"That's where Madame Mystic comes in,"

Wall Street answered. "That's where she uses her real powers."

"Real powers?" It was Opera's turn to squeak. "You've got a way for making locked doors fly open?"

"I certainly do." She reached into her pocket and pulled out a giant key ring full of keys. "My son Bartholomew is a locksmith, when he's not making and selling ghost-detector instruments to you. With these keys we will be able to get inside in no time."

Opera sighed in relief. "So we're just getting in the old-fashioned way?"

I mumbled, "Which means we'll just get thrown in jail the old-fashioned way."

"Look!" Wall Street pointed.

We all turned and watched as the living room light went off. A moment later, the kitchen light went off.

Now only one light remained, and it was off in the far corner—probably in the housekeeper's room.

We watched breathlessly, waiting nearly a minute, before it too went off.

"Okay," Wall Street said, rising to her feet. "Let's get in there and see what we've got."

Wall Street reached down and helped Madame Mystic stand.

But for some reason Opera and I felt a lot more comfortable staying on the ground, cowering under the bushes.

"Come on, guys," Wall Street said scornfully. "Don't be such chickens."

"Actually," Opera said, clearing his throat, "did you know the average life span of a live chicken is several times longer than that of a dead hero?"

"Guys!"

No way were we moving.

Wall Street crossed her arms. "So, Wally, does this mean you've lost the bet? That you're willing to admit there really are ghosts?"

I thought of what Mom and Mr. Figledoober had said about messing with this stuff. (I also thought of all that money I'd be losing, and the fact that I should not be betting in the first place.)

I looked up at Wall Street.

"'Cause if you don't go in," she said, grinning, "then you'll prove my point, and I'll win . . . just like always."

I hate it when she does that. Win, I mean.

So, with a groan, I slowly rose to my feet. It was the last thing I wanted to do, but after destroying the public library, Madame Mystic's place, and Mr. Figledoober's pet shop, I figured

Dad was about tapped out of money . . . at least for this week.

I reached down to Opera, who was still hiding.

"Come on," I said. "It won't be that bad."

He shook his head.

"Come on."

More head shaking.

Finally, I had to say what I had to say, and though I hated myself for saying it, I said it anyway.

TRANSLATION:
I was about to be a jerk.

"Besides," I said, "she might have some more chocolate chip cookies."

Immediately his eyes lit up and he leaped to his feet. I guess everyone has their price.

"Come on," Wall Street said, motioning us across the street.

"All right." I let out a heavy sigh as we started to follow. "But if we die, you're going to live to regret it."

Chapter 8

Break In!

We snuck up the porch stairs, which went out of their way to

> *Groan,*
> *Creak,* and
> *Squeak*

with every step we took.

Once we arrived, Madame Mystic pulled out her keys and was about to begin working on the lock when, ever so slowly, the door

> *K-Screeech . . .*

opened . . . all by itself.

Wall Street, Opera, and I

> Gasp . . . Gasp . . . **Gasp**ed

in perfect three-part harmony.

But not Madame Mystic. "It must be the wind. Everything has a natural explanation," she said.

Then she pushed the door open farther and motioned for us to follow. "Come."

Against my common sense (against anybody's common sense), we followed her through the doorway and into the blackness of the entry hall.

The place was dark, spooky, cold, spooky, and—did I mention spooky?

Then there were those coffins . . .

The good news was, they were not out on the porch. The bad news was, they were just inside the door.

But, of course, it wasn't the coffins that made me go cold with terror. It was what was inside them.

Madame Mystic saw the look on my face and reached out to the nearest coffin.

I tried to warn her, but I was too busy re-swallowing my heart.

Ever so gently, she tapped on the lid.

The good news was, there was no tapping back.

She frowned.

The bad news was, after she frowned, she pushed open the lid, reached her hand down to the corpse, and grabbed hold of its rotting arm!

Of course, the three of us repeated our symphony of multiple gasps.

And, of course, she didn't stop. Instead, she pulled the entire arm out of the coffin . . . and we did another encore performance.

"What are you doing?!" Wall Street whispered.

"Plastic," Madame Mystic said as she bent the arm. "It's all plastic."

"Plastic?" I whispered.

"Plastic," she said again, nodding. "Nothing supernatural or weird about it. Like I said, everything has a natural explanation."

"Unless . . ." Opera shivered.

"Unless what?"

"Unless the ghost turns you into plastic."

Madame Mystic looked at him and tapped the lid again. "While at the same time turning your coffin into plastic?"

"It could happen," Opera argued.

Wall Street reached out and touched the lid.

So did I.

Then she reached out and touched the body.

I didn't. (My name might be on the cover of this book, but I am no hero . . . or fool.)

"She's right," Wall Street said. "Everything's plastic."

Madame Mystic nodded. Then she repeated,

"Nothing is supernatural. Everything has a natural explanation."

I started to relax. Who knew what the Professor's housekeeper was doing with plastic bodies inside plastic caskets, but Madame Mystic had a point . . . there was nothing supernatural about it.

I just wish she could have said the same about the ball of light that suddenly appeared at the top of the stairway.

Opera was the first to see it, which would explain his

"AUGH!"

Next, Wall Street and I turned, which would explain our

"AUGH! **AUGH!**"

Madame Mystic spun around. The good news was, she didn't scream when she saw it. The bad news was, she started to shake.

The light grew brighter. Bigger. Soon it took on the shape of the old man we'd seen on the roof.

"It's Professor Grimm!" I whispered.

Madame Mystic repeated, "Everything has a

natural explanation, everything has a natural explanation."

Unfortunately, she was no longer talking to us, but to herself: "Everything has a natural explanation, everything has a natural explanation."

Opera nodded in agreement. "Like natural ghosts wanting to naturally kill us."

Wall Street nodded. "Naturally."

Wind began blowing the old man's tuxedo and long gray hair.

"Everything has a natural explanation," Madame Mystic repeated, "everything has a natural explanation. . . ."

Suddenly, Wall Street's Ghost Detector Recorder started to

WHIRRRrrr. . . .

"Look," she cried, "I'm picking up a ghost image."

"That's impossible," Madame Mystic argued. "That equipment is fake!"

Next, Opera's Ghost Detector Radar began to

beep-beep-beep-beep.

He looked up at us. "The ghost levels are off the chart!"

"That's impossible," Madame Mystic cried. "They're fake. All of this equipment is fake!"

The *whirr*ing grew louder, the *beep*ing shriller.

"You'll have to tell them that!" Wall Street said, pointing at the equipment.

Professor Grimm turned and glared down at us.

Madame Mystic took a nervous step backward.

I turned to her. "Ev-ev-everything has a natural explanation, r-r-right?"

She tried to nod.

She would have been more believable if her teeth weren't chattering so loudly. And even more believable if she wasn't continuing to inch backward toward the door.

Slowly, the ghost raised his arm until he pointed his bony finger directly at us. The wind blew so hard that chunks of his hair began flying away, then his tuxedo, then his body—just like they had on the roof.

Madame Mystic had reached the door. It was hard to tell in the light, but she looked as white as the Professor.

Soon the ghost was nothing but a skeleton . . . until even his bones crumbled and fell to the stairs, blowing away in the wind with absolutely no sound.

Well, actually there was one sound. . . .

The sound of Madame Mystic screaming for her life as she spun around, threw the door open, and ran down the porch steps.

Better make that two sounds . . .

The sound of the door slamming behind her as she ran down the porch steps screaming for her life.

Well, all right, there were actually three sounds . . . if you count the sound of a giant lock falling into place as the door slammed behind her as she ran down the porch steps screaming for her life.

Of course, there may have been even more, but it was hard to hear anything over my pounding heart, my gasping breath, and my pathetic whimpering.

Chapter 9

A Little House Tour

Ever notice when you're trapped inside a haunted house and pounding on the locked door to get out, that no amount of

*Bang, Bang, Bang*ing
or
*Scream, scream, scream*ing

seems to help? I've also noticed it's true when it comes to

*faint, faint, faint*ing.

So, after two or three hours of proving my point, I finally turned to Wall Street and cried, "What do we do?!"

She shook her head and looked up the stairs where the Professor's ghost had been standing.

"I can tell you one thing," she said, "I'm sure not going up there."

I nodded. It made perfect sense to me.

It would have made even more sense if the carpet we were standing on hadn't suddenly dropped out of sight.

Actually, the carpet dropping out of sight wasn't the problem. It was the three of us who had been standing on the carpet. The three of us who now dropped out of sight, sharing deep insights that went something like . . . how do I put it, oh, yes, now I remember:

"A u g h h h h !"   "A u g h h h h !"   "A u g h h h h !"

Unfortunately, that was the best part. Because—instead of falling forever into some nice and nasty dark dungeon—our luck got worse and we got sucked . . .

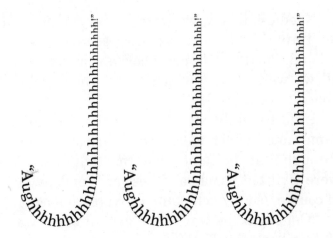

"Aughhhhhhhhhhhhhhhhhhh!"   "Aughhhhhhhhhhhhhhhh!"   "Aughhhhhhhhhhhhhhhhhhhhhh!"

up.

It's hard to explain, but it was like being in a giant elevator that dropped us for a second, then turned and shot us upward until we popped out at the second floor.

The good news was, we weren't anywhere near the top of the stairs where the ghost had been.

The bad news was, we were in some giant room with a dozen ghosts!

Yes sir, it was quite a collection. You name the ghosts and they were there—everything from your typical ghost in tattered clothes, to a pirate ghost, to one in a fluttering nightgown, to a flying ghost. And what collection would be complete without the ever-popular headless ghost (holding his own head, of course).

Needless to say, we were all very impressed. So impressed that we immediately spun around, spotted an open door, and ran to it for all we were worth (which at this moment was about 1½ cents).

Unfortunately, we all got to the door at the same time—which meant we all tried to squeeze through it at the same time. But that's okay. We were civilized people and best of friends, which, of course, led to such polite conversation as:

"Get out of the way!" "You get out of the way!" "I was here first!" "Move your elbow!" Let me through! You let *me* through. Who do you think you are! Let me in! You let me in! Will you just be quiet and let me get in ahead of you! I tell you, I was here first. What difference does that make? Let me through. You let me through. I was here first. No, you weren't. I was. Says who? Says me! Well, me doesn't count because I'm getting in there whether you like it or not so live with it. You live with it! Let me through! You let *me* through. Who do you think you are! Let me in! You let me in! Will you just be quiet and let me get in ahead of you! I tell you, I was here first. What difference does that make? Let me through. You let me through. I was here first. No, you weren't. I was. Says who? Says me! Well, me doesn't count because I'm getting in there. I tell you I was here first. What difference does that make? Let me through. You let me through. I was here first. No you weren't. I was. Says who? Says me! Well me doesn't count because I'm getting in there whether you like it or not so live with it. You live with it! Let me through! You let me through! Who do you think you are! Let me in! You let me in! Will you just be quiet and let me get in ahead of you! I think you are! Let me in! You let me in! Will you just be quiet and let me get in ahead of you! Let me through! You let me through! I was here first! No

Somehow, someway, we made it through the door without breaking any bones or leaving any major body parts behind.

That was the good news.

Unfortunately, as you've already guessed, there was also some bad news. . . .

Instead of a nice room with a dozen ghosts and ghouls, we were standing in a room that appeared to be a graveyard . . . complete with trees, hanging moss, and more than the daily minimum requirement of giant spiderwebs, which, of course, included more than the daily minimum requirement of giant spiders crawling toward us.

"GIANT SPIDERS CRAWLING TOWARD US??!!"

(Sorry, didn't mean to yell. I should have saved that

for all the ghosts shooting up out of their graves.)

"GHOSTS SHOOTING UP OUT OF THEIR GRAVES!!??!!"

(See what I mean?)

I looked at Opera and Wall Street.

Opera and Wall Street looked at me.

Voting for a new form of self-expression, we decided not to scream hysterically.

Instead, we broke out running . . . hysterically. This way and that. That way and this. (When you don't know where you're going, it really doesn't matter which way you're running . . . just as long as you're running.)

But all good things must come to an end. . . .

Opera was the first to trip, fall, and

"Aughhhhh . . ."

disappear.

Next, Wall Street disappeared. The same tripping, the same falling, and the same

"Aughhhhh . . ."ing.

That left yours truly. For the life of me (which would only be a few more seconds), I couldn't imagine what my friends had tripped over and fallen into. I mean, there were only these tombstones

K-Trip

and these open graves . . .

K-Fall

which brought me to the overused but always popular

"Aughhhhh. ..."

* * * * *

Believe me, there are worse things than falling into an open grave. (And as soon as I think of one I'll let you know.)

But this was no ordinary open grave. Oh, no, that would have been way too, er, uh . . . ordinary.

Instead, it was like another secret passageway. One that dropped Opera, Wall Street, and me into a glass cavern. It was pretty weird. The walls, floor, and ceiling all seemed to be made of mirrors. It was also pretty dark—except for the glowing bat eyes that hung all around us . . . and our own glowing bodies.

"Our own glowing bodies!"

(Sorry, I'm yelling again, aren't I?)

"Wally," Wall Street cried, "what's wrong with you?!"

I turned to her. Not only was she glowing, but she was sort of clear and transparent . . . just like the Professor's ghost had been!

"Me?!" I shouted. "What about you? I'm not the one with the ghost body!"

"Guess again," Opera said from behind me.

I spun around to see that he was also glowing and transparent—exactly like Wall Street!

"What's wrong with you two?!" I demanded.

"The same thing that's wrong with you!" Wall Street shouted. She pointed to the mirrors around us, and I looked at myself—well, what little of myself I could see. Because, sure enough, just like my friends, I was also glowing and transparent.

"We're ghosts!" Opera cried, staring at his own glowing body. "We've all died and become ghosts!"

"How can that be?" I demanded.

"Dumb luck?" Wall Street offered.

I reached down and touched my body. It felt solid enough. But the mirrors and my friends said something entirely different.

"How can this be?" I repeated. "There are no such things as ghosts!"

"If there are no such things as ghosts," Wall Street shouted back, "then there are no such things as us."

"What will we do?" I shouted.

"Where will we go?" Wall Street asked.

"What will we eat?" Opera complained.

"So many questions," a gravelly old voice chuckled from behind us.

We spun around and saw the Professor's ghost standing before us—so scary that we would have jumped out of our skin (if we had skin to jump out of).

He continued, "So, tell me, what do you think?"

Not wanting to be rude, I glanced around the cavern. "I, I really like what you've done with the place," I stuttered. "Early American Hades, isn't it?"

The ghost chuckled and moved closer.

"Please, Mr. Ghost," Opera whimpered, "I'm too young to die!"

"A little late for that," Wall Street muttered.

I would have added something equally as clever, but I noticed my shoe was untied. And, since the last thing you want to do is float around haunting houses for eternity with an untied shoe, I bent over and tied it.

That's when I noticed everyone's feet. From down below they all looked perfectly normal, completely solid. Even the Professor's shoes looked real.

I frowned.

Wall Street's feet were the closest, so I reached out and touched them.

Of course she screamed, which of course made me leap to the side.

Well, "to the side" was the direction I tried to leap. Instead, I crashed into some sort of glass curtain that hung invisibly all around me from the ceiling to about a foot off the floor.

Well, it had hung invisibly. Now it started to

K-crack, K-crack, K-crack!

I watched as little lines shot out in all directions. First, they spread across my glass curtain (which completely surrounded me). Next, they spread to Wall Street's glass curtain (which completely surrounded her), then over to Opera's, and finally to the Professor's.

And once they had *K-crack, K-crack, K-cracked*, they started to fall and

K-crash, K-crash, K-crash.

As they did, our glows disappeared. So did our transparency. Now we were all completely normal. (Well, *they* were all completely normal. I was still, you know, Wally McDoogle.)

But the show wasn't quite over yet. . . .

With the crashing of the glass curtains, lights began to flicker on. Suddenly, I noticed we were not in an underground cavern, but in a laboratory! A laboratory with more computers and flashing lights than NASA's Mission Control!

"LOOK WHAT YOU'VE DONE!" the Professor shouted over the *K-crashing*. "LOOK WHAT YOU'VE DONE TO ALL MY HARD WORK!"

"WORK?" Wall Street yelled.

But it was hard to hear much over all the noise (and my hysterical screaming).

"QUICKLY!" the Professor said, motioning. "FOLLOW ME! EVERYTHING'S SHORTING OUT!"

"WHAT?!" we shouted.

Suddenly, a giant chunk of the ceiling

*K-SMASH*ed and
*tinkle, tinkle, tinkl*ed

onto the floor.

"IT'S BLOWING UP!" he shouted. "FOLLOW ME OUTSIDE WHERE IT'S SAFE!"

Now, the Professor, or ghost, or whoever he was, didn't exactly seem like the safest person on the block. But at the moment, he seemed the smartest.

"HURRY!" He motioned us toward some distant stairs. "IT'S ALL COMING DOWN!!"

So, not wanting to be a spoilsport (or a dead one), I decided to play along. I raced behind him, dodging the falling mirrors, the glass curtains, and any other opportunity to crash into something.

The only thing I didn't dodge was some weird purple beam shooting out of a weirder purple machine. Everyone else managed to sidestep it, except yours truly . . . which would explain the

K-ZIP . . . K-ZAP . . .
K-ZIP-A-DEE-DOO-DAH!

that always happens when your entire body is changed into a giant hamburger!

"A GIANT HAMBURGER??!!"
(I'm doing it again. Sorry.)

The good news was, I still had my arms and legs . . . and I couldn't taste any of the pickles. (I hate pickles.)

The bad news was, the pickles were on top of my head, acting as my eyes. (Don't you just hate it when that happens?)

"WALLY!" Wall Street shouted. "WHAT HAPPENED?!"

I tried to answer, but it's hard to say much when your tongue has turned into a 100 percent USDA beef patty!

Luckily, I was able to run.

Unluckily, I couldn't see where I was running. (Pickles don't make for great eyes.)

"HURRY!" the Professor kept shouting. "HURRY!"

Wall Street guided me to the stairs, and we ran down them as fast as we could. Actually, faster than we could, thanks to

K-Thud
"Ow!"

my slipping,

K-Bamb
"Ouch!"

rolling,

K-Slam
"Watch it!"

and hitting everyone I knew along the way.

Chapter 10

Wrapping Up

We finally staggered outside onto the front lawn.

I was glad all three of us had escaped with our lives. (Or four of us, if you count the Professor's ghost. By the way, how does a ghost escape with his life?)

Of course, I would have been happier if "escaping with my life" didn't also involve me becoming a beef patty, tomato slice, lettuce, special sauce, and a sesame-seed bun. But, being the cool and collected guy that I am, I calmly evaluated the situation and immediately started running in every direction I could think of.

"Wally!" Wall Street yelled.

"Wally!" Opera shouted. "Come back!"

But I wasn't in the mood for listening to anyone, especially to Opera (who hadn't eaten in thirty-nine minutes and was already eyeing me hungrily). So, instead of behaving like any normal, in-between-meals snack, I continued running crazily until I—

K-Splat!

hit a friendly nearby tree.

A friendly nearby tree that had the courtesy to send me off into the land of unconsciousville.

* * * * *

When I woke up, Wall Street, Opera, and the ghost were all staring down at me.

"Are you all right?" Wall Street asked.

I nodded and immediately checked my head. As best I could tell, I was no longer a fast-food item. I had returned to my normal self.

"What . . . what happened?" I asked.

The ghost answered, "My Matter Transference Beam momentarily changed the molecular structure of your more superficial surfaces."

"Your what did how to who?"

Before he could answer me, the old housekeeper came running out of the house. "Oh, Professor," she cried as she raced down the porch steps to join us. "You're alive!"

"Yes, Bertha, I'm fine."

She ran into his arms, and he gave her a polite hug. Then, turning back to the house, he added, "I just wish I could say the same thing about my lab."

We all turned and watched as the last of the smoke rose from the second-story windows.

"Your lab?" Opera asked nervously. "What does a ghost need with a lab?"

"A ghost?" the man asked.

Wall Street nodded. "We read about your death in the paper. The car crash a few years back."

"Car crash?" He frowned a moment, then seemed to understand. "No, no, no, that wasn't me who died. That was my brother."

"Your brother?"

"The other Professor Grimm. We were partners until his death."

"But we saw you," Wall Street argued. "Up on that roof, and later on the stairs—doing your, you know, ghost thing."

"Yeah," Opera added. "Until you turned into a skeleton and blew off into a cloud of dust."

He shook his head. "You saw a holographic image of me."

"A holo who?"

"I design rides for amusement parks."

"Like roller coasters and stuff?" Wall Street asked.

"What do ghosts need roller coasters for?" Opera asked.

"I'm *not* a ghost. I'm a scientist who specializes in horror rides and haunted house attractions. That projection you saw of me was one of my latest inventions. That and the Crypt Room you just destroyed."

"Crypt Room?" I asked.

"Using the latest digital equipment, I simultaneously captured your images, computer-generated them, and projected them back onto the glass curtains surrounding you."

"Making us *look* like ghosts?" Wall Street asked.

"Exactly."

"And my hamburger imitation?" I asked, spitting out a sesame seed.

"An entirely different approach, but one that can have equally startling effects."

"You mean like scaring us to death," I said.

"Well, yes." He grinned. "That is the idea."

"So everything was fake?" Wall Street asked. "Just illusions?"

The Professor nodded. "Simply the latest in scientific technology."

"I'm sorry about all of the damage we did," I said.

"Damage *you* did," Wall Street corrected me.

The Professor shrugged. "These things happen."

I looked at the ground. "With me, more than you can imagine."

He put his hand on my shoulder. "Well, at least you're not Wally McDoogle. I hear his life is one nonstop catastrophe."

I looked up, startled. "I *am* Wally McDoogle."

The Professor's eyes widened. Now *he* looked like *he'd* seen a ghost. "*You're* Wally McDoogle?"

I nodded.

"I can't believe it. Did you know I spent all last year trying to design a theme park ride around your life?"

"I thought you did horror rides," I said.

"Exactly!" he agreed.

"So, what happened?" Wall Street asked.

"It always ended with the ride blowing up."

I nodded, knowing exactly how he felt.

"Listen," he said, growing more and more excited. "Would you come back into the house? I'd love to show you my plans. Maybe you can give me some insight into what to do."

"What about the haunted house ride?" I asked.

He looked back at the remains of his second-story lab. "I'm afraid that's a lost cause. At least for now. But if I could pick your brain . . . well, who knows, maybe we could replace it with a *Wally McDoogle Horror Ride* instead!"

I looked at Wall Street. "What do you think?"

She shrugged. "If there's money, count me in."

I looked at Opera.

"If there are ghosts, count me out."

"Opera, there are *no* ghosts," I exclaimed.

"Says who?"

"Says the Professor!"

Opera shrugged. "Sorry, but I've never been too good at trusting a ghost's word."

Then Bertha had an idea. "What if I bake a batch of those chocolate chip cookies that you liked so much?"

Now she had his attention.

"What if she bakes a double batch?" Wall Street asked.

Now he doubled his attention. "With walnuts?"

We all nodded.

"What are we waiting for?" Opera turned and started for the porch steps.

"What about the ghosts?" I asked.

"Do they eat chocolate chip cookies?" Opera asked.

"I don't think so," I answered.

"Then that leaves more for us! Come on!"

With that bit of logic, we headed back into the house.

It was important I give the Professor a hand. After destroying his lab, I figured the least I could do was help where I could.

After going forty-two and a half minutes without a snack, Opera figured the least he could do was eat what he could.

And after losing her bet with me (a first for the history books!), Wall Street figured the least she could do was make money where she could. And, of course, her mind was already spinning.

"Excuse me, Professor," she said. "Since we're talking about amusement park rides . . ."

"Yes," the Professor said as we started up the porch steps.

"How about a *McDoogle Merry-Go-Round?*"

"How would that work?"

"Simple. It goes out of control and spins faster and faster until everyone gets thrown off," Wall Street said.

The Professor nodded politely. "Hmm . . ."

"Or a *Wally Parachute Ride* where the kids jump off the platform and the parachutes never open."

"I see."

Good ol' Wall Street. She may have been wrong about ghosts, but she was still on her way to making that first million. And, as always, it would be off me.

* * * * *

It was pretty late by the time I got home. Normally, Dad would have been mad. But when I told him the Professor was so grateful for my help that he wasn't going to charge us for blowing up his lab . . . suddenly he was all smiles.

I, on the other hand, was so wound up about the day that I knew I couldn't sleep. So, grabbing Ol' Betsy, I decided to finish up my Manners Man story. . . .

When we last left Manners Man and Rude Dude, they were about to make a major impression on the road outside the hospital window.

But as luck would have it (along with more great writing from a great writer), someone had left the manhole cover off. So, instead of your typical

Ker-Splat! Ker-Splat!

there was the less typical

Ker-Splash! Ker-Splash!

of two superguys landing in a storm drain. And the even more unusual...

glug, glug, glug

of one of them drowning.

"May I ask what's wrong?!" Manners Man shouts over the roaring water.

"I'm, *glug, glug, glug,* drowning, you minimind!"

"Well, you certainly don't have to be rude about it!" Manners Man shouts.

"I can't help my, *glug, glug, glug,* self. Rudy's broadcast beam is too, *glug, glug, glug,* powerful. He must be very, *glug, glug, K-LANK,* close."

"Wait a minute, did you just K-LANK when you should have glugged?"

"I'm not sure. I think, *K-LANK, K-LANK, K-LANK,* so!"

"Great Grandma's Green Beans!" our hero shouts. "We're next to a minisub!"

"But not just any, *K-LANK, K-LANK, K-LANK,* minisub!" Rude Dude cries. "It's Rudy the Robot's sub!"

Grabbing a hatch on the passing sub, Manners Man opens it and they both

K-thud, K-thud

fall inside (with about five gazillion gallons of water).

That's the good news.

The better news is, Rudy is standing just below them.

(Talk about great writing!)

The best news is, as the water
pours onto him, he immediately

K-zap, K-spark

shorts himself out into Robot Heaven.

And, as his power fades (making
this the quickest superhero ending of
all time—I told you I was good!), the
worldwide rudeness disappears.

"Wow!" Rude Dude shouts. "That was
wondrous work, Manners Man!"

"Why, thank you, Rude Dude. But I
simply could not have done it without
your assistance."

"You mean we worked together as a
team?"

"Yes, and it's been quite a pleasure."

"Why, thank you, Manners Man."

"You're certainly welcome, Rude Dude."

"Excuse me, Manners Man?"

"Yes, Rude Dude?"

"Would you mind if we closed that hatch now? If any more water pours in, I'll have to resume my drowning routine."

"And that would be unpleasant?"

"Yes, I believe so."

And so, as the two work together to

K-REEEAK

close the hatch, they begin talking about other problems they can solve. Important world issues like:

—Insisting thieves say please and thank you when they hold up banks.
—Teaching pigs how to properly tie napkins around their necks before dining.
—And, of course, encouraging all bullies to politely ask for permission before they pulverize your face or body.

All this as the sub slowly sails into the sunset (a neat trick when it's

underwater), leaving the world a far
more courteous and polite place to live.

I looked at the screen and winced. On the
McDoogle Schlock Scale of 1 to 10, this was an
easy 19.3. Still, I suppose it had a pretty good
message. I mean, people are getting kinda rude
these days.

Anyway, after shutting Ol' Betsy down and
changing into my pajamas (where I noticed I
still had some tomato and lettuce in my underwear), I hopped into bed, ready for a little peace
and quiet. Until my phone began to

$$\text{\$\$\$ I want your money! \$\$\$}$$
$$\text{\$\$\$ I want your money! \$\$\$}$$

ring.

Apparently, my little misadventures weren't
entirely over. Not by a long shot.

$$\text{\$\$\$ I want your money! \$\$\$}$$
$$\text{\$\$\$ I want your money! \$\$\$}$$

A *very* long shot.

Another BILL MYERS series!

Who knew that the old rock found forgotten in the attic was actually the key to a fantastic alternative world? When Denise, Nathan, and Joshua stumble into the land of Fayrah, ruled by the Imager—the One who makes us in His image—they are drawn into wonderful adventures that teach them about life, faith, and the all-encompassing heart of God.

Book 1: THE PORTAL
(ISBN: 1-4003-0744-9)
Denise and Nathan meet a myriad of interesting characters in the wondrous world they've just discovered, but soon Nathan's selfish nature—coupled with some tricky moves by the evil Illusionist—gets him imprisoned. Denise and her new friends try desperately to free Nathan from the villain, but one of them must make an enormous sacrifice—or they will all be held captive!

Book 2: THE EXPERIMENT
(ISBN: 1-4003-0745-7)
Amateur scientist Josh unexpectedly finds himself whisked away to Fayrah with Denise. Quickly, he sees that not every-

thing can be explained rationally as he watches Denise struggle to grasp the enormity of the Imager's love. It's not until they meet the Weaver—who weaves the threads of God's plan into each life—that they both discover that understanding takes an element of faith.

Book 3: THE WHIRLWIND
(ISBN: 1-4003-0746-5)
The mysterious stone transports the three friends to Fayrah, where they find themselves caught between good and evil. There Josh falls under the spell of the trickster Illusionist and his henchman Bobok—who convince him that he can become perfect. Before they lose Josh in the Sea of Justice, Denise and Nathan must enlist the help of someone who is truly perfect. Will help come in time?

Book 4: THE TABLET
(ISBN: 1-4003-0747-3)
Denise finds a tablet with mysterious powers, and she is beguiled by the chance to fulfill her own desires—instead of trusting the Imager's plan. But when Josh and Nathan grasp the danger she faces, they work desperately to stop the Merchant of Emotions before he destroys Denise—and the whole world!

Guys (and Guyettes)!

Want to hear from me,
the Human Walking Disaster Area,
each week about more misadventures
and the stuff I'm learning in the Bible?

There'll also be riddles to solve
and chances to win prizes!

Log on to www.BillMyers.com and click
on the Wally McDoogle Fan Club icon for
more information and how to join!

Hope to hear from ya!

Wally